# THE LITTLE TREE GROWIN' IN THE SHADE

# THE LITTLE TREE GROWIN' IN THE SHADE

## CAMILLE YARBROUGH

ILLUSTRATED BY
## TYRONE GETER

G. P. PUTNAM'S SONS · NEW YORK

G. P. Putnam's Sons, a division of The Putnam & Grosset Group.

200 Madison Avenue, New York, NY 10016.

G. P. Putnam's Sons, Reg. U. S. Pat. & Tm. Off.

Published simultaneously in Canada.

Printed in Hong Kong by South China Printing Co. (1988) Ltd

Designed by Donna Mark.

Text set in Sabon.

Library of Congress Cataloging-in-Publication Data

Yarbrough, Camille. Little tree growing in the shade /

Camille Yarbrough ; illustrated by Tyrone Geter.   p.   cm.

Summary: A young African American brother and sister learn how

their people came to be enslaved, how they managed to retain

their cultural identity despite the many hardships they suffered,

and how they finally gained their freedom.

[1. Afro–Americans—History—Fiction.   2. Slavery—Fiction.

3. Brothers and sisters—Fiction.]   I. Geter, Tyrone, ill.   II. Title.

PZ7.Y1955Li   1996   [Fic]—dc20   95-23610   CIP   AC

ISBN 0-399-21204-3

1 3 5 7 9 10 8 6 4 2

First Impression

*To the Ancestors*
—C.Y.


*This book is dedicated to the many voices who
heard the music and understood its message,
making enormous sacrifice in the struggle
for human dignity and freedom.*
—T.G.

I'm tellin' you, sometimes little brothers are a lot of fun, but sometimes they don't know how to act. My little brother used to follow me around everywhere and do everything I did. He doesn't do that anymore. Now he's doin' somethin' else.

Now he's a deep sleeper, and he is always sleepin' deep at the wrong time. Like, Sunday we were supposed to go to a music concert in the park. The music was going to be some songs called spirituals, and Daddy promised to tell us a story about um. But you know what happened? We were takin' our naps. Then Mama called us. She said. "Brother! Sister! It's time to get up so we can go to the concert."

I got up real fast but Brother was movin' real slow, so I got to the bathroom first and washed up and put on my clothes and everything. When I came out I called him to come on and use the bathroom 'cause I'm finished. Then I helped Great-Grammaw put on her shawl and then went on up to the second floor to help Mr. Witherspoon come down the stairs to our apartment, so he could go to the concert with us. Mr. Witherspoon is ninety-six years old and he doesn't have any family left, so he adopted us and we adopted him.

When we came downstairs, Mama told us to come on in the kitchen. She and Daddy were takin' the foldin' stools and sittin' pillows out of the closet. Then Mama looked around. She said, "Where's Brother?"

Everybody looked around but nobody saw him. He wasn't in the kitchen with us. He wasn't in the front room and he wasn't in the bathroom. You know where he was? He was still in the bed, deep sleepin'. I told Daddy, "Daddy, we ought to leave Brother home 'cause he doesn't know how to act." But Daddy said we have to help him along till he can do better.

Great-Grammaw went into the bedroom to get him up and we heard her say, "Brother, if you don't get up out of that bed you better!" Then we heard ol' Brother say, "I'm up, Great-Grammaw. I'm up!" Then he came walkin' out into the hall lookin' like the mummy we saw on television last week. He had the clean clothes Mama had pressed for him all balled up in his arms and he was walkin' but he was still sleepin' 'cause his eyes were closed. Daddy took him into the bathroom and got him together. When they came out, ol' Brother put his baseball cap on the same way Daddy wears his bicycle cap and said, "Come on, everybody, we don't want to be late." I couldn't believe it. I'm telling you! Anyway, we finally went to the park.

It's just around the corner from our house and when we got there, people were everywhere, sellin' home-made food and clothes and jewelry, buyin' and eatin' and drinkin' cool drinks and stylin' their summer clothes, and having a good time dancin' to the music from their radios. And you know what, it seemed like everybody knew Daddy. All the musicians and singers were glad to see him. He used to play music with them before he started teachin' school, and they hugged him and kissed him and shook his hand and Mr. Witherspoon's hand and kissed Mama and Great-Grammaw and Brother and me. When the musicians went up on the stage, we all sat down on our foldin' stools and pillows right in front on the grass where we could hear the music and see what was happenin' too. There was a big sign sayin' THE ROOTS OF RHYTHM AND BLUES hangin' up over the stage, and a whole lot of lights were hangin' up there too on long pipes. It was almost dark night but the lights were real dim. Then the people in the crowd started clappin' all together 'cause they wanted the musicians to start playin' live music, and the lights came on bright and they were all different colors, and when the

musicians played their trumpets and saxophones and trombones and flutes, the lights made them look like real gold and silver and made streaks in the dark like colored sparklin' diamonds. The bass player was huggin' his big bass and the drummer and the piano player were playin' so fast we could hardly see their hands. Music was everywhere. *Tume tume pata tume tume, tume tume pata tume tume, be pata tume, be pata tume, tume tume pata tume tume tume.*

I was sittin' on a pillow on one side of Daddy, and Brother was sittin' on a pillow on the other side. Daddy was sittin' on a stool, and he put his arms around us and pulled us up close to him and whispered to us, "The singer we're going to hear specializes in songs called African-American or Negro spirituals."

I said, "Spirituals? Why are they called spirituals?"

"The answers to your questions," Daddy told me, "are in the story I'm going to tell you. I call it 'The Story of the Little Tree Growin' in the Shade.' "

"Tell it," Brother said, "tell it, Daddy."

"Well." Daddy cleared his throat. "Our story begins at the beginning," he said softly. "Way way back, in a time not remembered, at a place called the Rift Valley on the continent called Africa, the tree of life grew to its fullness, and for the first time humans who could talk, think, create, love, worship and who walked up tall on two feet came into being. Centuries passed. Their numbers increased. Many of them left their birthplace in that valley in East Africa and traveled to distant continents. Others who stayed in the mother valley, nourished by the mother tree, gradually spread out over the land to the north, the south, the west. And as life continued, they developed and blossomed into culturally rich and inventive nations of people, people who in the coming years would give so much to humankind. Their power and glory lasted a long time, but in life, you know, power and glory come and go, and so by and by a storm of tragedy came to that land, to those people. A storm of creaking slave ships heavy with cannons and men with cutlasses and guns. A storm of slavery sent by some of the rulers on the continent of Europe who needed money to build up their countries. 'We can make money from the free labor of slaves,' their advisers told them. 'We can make money selling slaves in the new lands that we hear are beyond the seas.' And so they sent their slave ships to Africa. And the storm of slavery rose, first clouding the west coast of Africa in the year 1441. Then it broke, and for four centuries it grew and raged, destroying and tearing a great branch from the mother tree, a branch of millions of African peoples who were captured, enslaved, put into the cruel cannon ships and sailed away from their homes, far far away.

"Many of the people were taken to the lands that we now call the Caribbean islands, South and Central America and finally many millions more were sold to the north, to the land that would become the United States of America, where the last captured smuggler slave ship lowered its moaning sails and came to rest in Mobile Bay, Alabama, in the year 1859. That torn branch of millions of African peoples, scattered throughout those lands, brought their ancient and rich cultures with them."

Brother said, "I bet they had lots of suitcases when they came off the ships, Daddy, just like that rich movie star did. Remember, we saw her

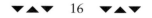

on the news last night comin' off the ship with all those suitcases?"

"Ouuu, snap, Brother, that's not funny," I said. "You're makin' fun of our ancestors. You know they didn't come off those ol' slaver ships carryin' suitcases."

He told me, "Well, Daddy said they were rich, didn't he, Sister?"

I told him, "He said they had a rich culture. He wasn't talkin' about suitcases and money and stuff."

Then ol' Brother put his hands on his no-hips and said, "That's why they had the suitcases, Sister. They had to carry all that rich culture in something, didn't they?"

I couldn't deal with it. I crossed my arms, laid back on the grass, looked up at the stars in the sky and listened to the music. The drummer was playin' a solo. *Pam pom pom pa-tum, pam pom pom pa-tum.*

Daddy was laughin'. When he stopped, he told me, "Brother doesn't know." Then he told ol' Brother, "The people were the suitcases."

Brother said, "Huh?" *Pam pom pom pa-tum, pam pom pom pa-tum.* The drummer was serious.

"You want to know what they brought with them?" Daddy asked.

"Tell me, Daddy," ol' Brother whispered. *Chinka ching, chinka ching, chinka ching, ching ching.* The drummer was doing it.

"Sister," Daddy called me. "You're the oldest, why don't you help your little brother find some answers?"

"Aww, Daddy!" I had to sit up.

"Didn't you write a school paper on culture?" he asked me.

"That assignment was way last year," I tried to tell him. He just looked at me and said, "See how much of it you can remember, big girl."

Ol' Brother stretched out on the grass with his arms folded, lookin' up at the stars imitatin' me, so I didn't pay him any mind. I just tried to remember what the teacher told us and what I wrote on my paper, and I talked to Daddy. "It's kind of hard to explain," I told him. "First, the teacher told us that all the different peoples of the world create cultures and that some expressions of their culture are the music they create, the things they believe in, their languages, the way they speak them."

"Right!" Daddy smiled. "Can we see words when people talk?" he asked. "Can we see the music the musicians are playing up there on the stage?"

We all looked up at the guitar player doing his solo in the spotlight. I said, "No, we can't see the music and we can't see words."

"But they do exist, don't they?" he asked. "Well, that's the kind of cultural baggage our African ancestors carried here with them. They were not allowed to bring the outside things of culture, things they made that could be seen. But they brought the inside things of culture. In their minds and bodies they carried their creative life-force energy—you see what I'm saying?—their way of thinking, understanding, of doing things and feeling about life and living. They brought their religions, their dreams, their beliefs, languages, dances, styles, music, memories, imaginations, and thousands of years of learned wisdom and traditions which had guided them through life. That was the cultural baggage they carried inside them, Brother."

"I remember now," Brother said, bouncin' up and down, " 'cause that time when those dancers came to our school, they told us about culture and the slave ships and everything. I just forgot, that's all, and I wasn't tryin' to be funny, Sister, but you don't know everything all the time."

"I didn't say I did," I told him.

"Well, you're always showin' off, tellin' everything. You're not the teacher."

"I'm your big sister," I tried to tell him, "and the big ones are supposed to teach the little ones, so you have to listen to me."

"No, I don't." He sucked his teeth.

"Yes, you do too." I sucked my teeth.

"No, I DON'T NEITHER!" He wagged his head.

"Yes, you do so." I wagged my head. "And I'm tellin' you something I know, so snap on you."

"Snap on you back," the little ol' thing tried to say, but Mama put her finger out and told us, "That's the last of the snaps or I'm going to do

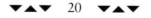

some snapping around here. I thought you wanted to hear the story."

"We do, Mama," we said.

"Then get it together," Daddy told us. "What's the last thing I told you?"

"About the branch of millions of African peoples that the slavers broke off the old African tree. About how they carried their culture inside of them when they were brought to the new lands," I told him.

"But Daddy," Brother whispered, "when does the story about the little tree growin' in the shade come in?"

"Right now, little man," Daddy whispered back. "When that broken-off branch of African people was brought here, it was like a weak and doomed little tree thrown down in the dirt of slavery, at the bottom of everything, trying to take hold in the shadow of the shade where the warmth and light of humanity could hardly be found. But the little-tree African people didn't give up down there. Soon after they arrived, they shared with one another some of the wisdom of their proverbs.

If a little tree grows in the shade
of a large tree,
the little tree will die little

warned the Wolof people. The warning of the proverb was quickly spread by those who spoke more than one language. Each language group added their thoughts to the proverb.

"In this land," a Bambara elder counseled,
"we are like the tree in the proverb,
   weak and small.
   If we are unable to find space for our roots to take hold
   or to feel the encouraging light of the sun,
   it is a rule of survival that we will
   wither and not grow at all."
"But," some Ga people added,
"the rule will not apply when the spirit won't die."

"And we refuse to die small," they all agreed.
"For we are a branch of the tree of life," the word spread,
"The mother tree of all."
"Don't worry," declared people from the Congo,
"we will use our culture to make space
  for our roots to take hold.
  We will be like the wise inchworm and rabbit we see here
  and we will live. Slavery will die.
  Remember," the Wolof said,
"a tree may fall into water
  and remain there a very long time
  but it will never become a crocodile."

"And so the little-tree African people used their cultural roots to make growing space for themselves. The first root they used was the spirit root. They were very spiritual people and believed in a great spirit God. Their great spirit God was serious and cool and bad. Back home in Africa they had many praise names for the great spirit God. Names like The Giver of Light, The Chief of Chiefs, The King of Kings, The Immovable Rock That Never Dies."

Mr. Witherspoon said, "Tell it."

Daddy kept namin'. "The Savior God," he said. "The God Who Walks with You and Sets Things in Order." Daddy clapped his hands.

"Make it clear." Mr. Witherspoon smiled, rockin' on his foldin' stool.

"They believed that the great spirit God could do anything, knew everything and was everywhere, and that the great spirit God had helper gods all around who could be heard and seen and felt in the *kaboom* of thunder, the *kre krack krack* of lightning, the *plim plam plum* of raindrops, the hum and splash of rivers, in the mist and color of rainbows, everywhere." Daddy whispered, "But you know what? There was a special place where the life spirit of the great God lived."

"Where, Daddy?" Brother asked.

"They believed," Daddy whispered, "that the life spirit of the great God lived in the words and sounds of human beings. For example, they believed that God's life spirit passes from you to me and from me back to you when we say words or sing them or hum or moan and things. See what I'm saying? And if something went bad, those old Africans believed they could help change it right back to good by saying and singing their spirit words and sounds."

"I bet they were singin' all the time," I told Daddy, " 'cause something tired is always happenin'."

Daddy nodded his head. "Yes," he whispered. "That's why they organized all kinds of festivals, ceremonies, rituals and rites to keep things in balance and to guide one another through each important step of life from birth to death. Some of the ceremonies started at sunup day and lasted through moon-bright night. Those were the special times when people sang and said their spirit power words to the helper gods who took them to the great spirit God.

"Let me give you a little taste of the kinds of songs they sang. They sang dirges, dialogues, death literature and all kinds of dramatic verse." Daddy sounded like he was singin' the words with the music. He said:

> They sang announcements, boasting poems, calls,
> challenge songs, courtship songs and
> the mighty curse.
> They sang legends, laments, lullabies, libations, love songs,
> recitations of law and speeches in the imperative, fables,
> histories and epic narratives.
> They sang oaths and prayers and proverbs, puns, riddles,
> rhymes, rhetoric, songs of ridicule and ritual dramas,
> myths, monologues, magic formulae, marriage
> and medicinal poetry and of course songs praising mamas.
> They sang tales and tongue-twister songs for teaching use
> salutations, songs of satire, social comment
> and songs for signifying abuse.

Someone in back of us said, "Talk that talk, mister."

"Daddy, you're marvelous," I whispered in his ear. "My teacher told us that when African people meet, sometimes it takes them half a day just to say 'how do' and ask how the family is. She said the human voice is the most used musical instrument in all of Africa."

Daddy smiled. "See what I'm saying? Everyone sang, soloists, duos, trios, quartets, whole communities sang and prayed together. At night around a fire, or in the daytime under a talk tree, some storyteller would dramatize a lesson story, singing and speaking

as fast as a jackhammer talkin'
or real slow and easy
like a contented turtle walkin'.
They stuttered, you know,
groaned, shouted, moaned
and like circling bees they would hum.
They syncopated, repeated and rhythmized their song words,
playing the air like a drum.

Daddy was preaching now.

Dirge and lament singers
half talked, half sang their sad songs of life
and death whisper soft
or as bass deep loud as a thunder rumble
and, when the proud hunter sang imitating sounds
of the forest, ouuu, they could make a mockingbird shame
and head bowed humble.

Traveling entertainer griots thumbed their coras
and made up songs for pay.
While history-singing griots
who would die before they'd lie
boasted, "No one can buy the truths I say."
And when priests and priestesses rhapsodized
in solemn dignity their song and wail
like the summer breeze and winter gale,
warming, chilling, low keyed, high pitched,
easy, tense, awesome in flight,
made the people feel as one
and helped change wrong to right.

Brother said, "All right," and he and Daddy slapped five.

"But," Daddy shook his head, "that's how it was over in Africa. Now over here, ouuu, the little-tree African people were in a bad situation, weren't they?

"You are property, not people," the slave laws instructed them.
"You cannot keep your religions.
   No more festivals, rituals or rites.
   No more African languages or dances.
   No more praying and singing through the night.
   No more families. No schools.
   No more playing of the drums.
   Only work from can-see to can't,
   then eat and rest till first light comes."
That was the law in the slave states.

"That was mean," Brother said.

Daddy nodded. "You know what the little-tree African people did then, Brother?"

Brother folded his arms. "I bet they didn't take no stuff," he answered.

"They did the best they could," Daddy told us. "For years thousands of them ran away and escaped to the free states or to Canada. And they were always breaking their work tools by mistake on purpose and working as slowly as they could get away with. Some like Nat Turner went to war with the slavers. But there was one thing all the little-tree African people did. And that's where the spirituals came in. They all used their spirit power words in song. You see, because anyone who was caught

'talkin' African' was whipped or killed or sold away somewhere, they had to learn to speak English hurry-up. In the beginning they learned to understand the orders and directions of the overseers and owners. But by listening carefully to everything that was said around them, they picked up more words to express what they thought and wanted to say. They spoke with African accents and put their words together in an African way. Then they used their spirit power in their new words to help change their bad condition back to good."

Ol' Brother looked at me. He was real serious now. I looked up to Daddy. On the stage the guitar player was playin'. *Kwwwwwang, kwa kwang kwang, kwwwwwwwwang, kwa kwang kwang.* "Then what did the little-tree African people do, Daddy?" I asked.

"First they put their words on the grapevine," Daddy whispered.

"Talk together. Plan a trick," they said.
"Point da straight way with a crooked stick.
  Hide away a pitch torch light,
  then slip to da woods an' swamp at night.
  Wet quilts an' rags hung in a square,
  keep da voice from trabblin' da air.
  Den you can plan, sing an' shout
  an' no ear will hear what words come out,"
  they whispered on the grapevine.
  And at night on the slave-worked plantation lands
  when candles and cookin' fires were put out,
  when guarding patrollers watched the roads
  and the people in the big houses slept,

▼▲▼ 34 ▼▲▼

then quiet like moon crossing sky,

like fog gliding lake,

those down at the bottom

little-tree African people

slipped from their cabins and from

shadow to shadow crept

to the praise house chosen for that night.

There they quickly turned an iron kettle down

with the mouth open to the dirt floor

so not a sound could be heard past the praise house door.

There they greeted one another, embracing, bowing, saluting in the
old country ways. They gave praise to the great spirit God and to
the helper gods, Legba, Eshu, Shango, Oshun and others. They
talked of home, loneliness and fear, of being

> whipped and maimed,
> of families taken, gone,
> friends gone,
> gone to the ancestors or
> gone, sold away.
> "Jula! Jula!" some spoke firmly. "Pull up! Jula! Pull up!
> Harrambi! Pull together. Jazzo! With energy!"

And then, just as the presence of a golden glow arching the night
   horizon announces the coming of the rising sun, so a deep
   rumbling moan trembled their bodies and rolled up and out from
   their throats like a sound storm, swirling in the room, surrounding
   them, calming them, releasing the pain from their worn and bruised
   bodies, pushing, pressing, squeezing despair and sorrow out from
   their hearts,
out through cracked, crude log walls, through broken plank roofs.

Out making way, announcing the coming of the spirit power words.
  And their spirit power breathed their new English words in song,
  bent them, squeezed them, worried them, reshaped and fixed them
  into old African melodies. On the sides of the rooms two and three
  people clapped, stomped rhythm and slowly began to sing
  while others in the center of the floor
  bent and formed a dancing, praying, shouting ring.

The leader sang

*Cum by heah, Lord*
*cum by heah*

and the ring shouted

*Cum by heah, Lord*
*cum by heah*
*cum by heah, Lord*
*cum by heah.*

and everyone sang

*Oh Lord, cum by heah*
*Somebody's prayin', Lord*
*cum by heah*
*Somebody's prayin', Lord*
*cum by heah*
*Somebody's praying', Lord*
*cum by heah*
*Oh Lord, cum by heah*

"And that's one of the ways the first spiritual songs were created," Daddy said. "Many years later, one of the little-tree African people who had been born into slavery told reporters:

Us ol' heads use ter make 'um on da spur of da moment after we russel wid da spirit an' come thru. But da tunes was brung from Africa by our elders. Dey was gis familiar songs . . . dey calls 'um spirituals, 'cause da holy spirit done revealed 'um to 'um.

Then she said:

Ah'd jump up dar an den holler an' shout an' sing an' pat an' dey would all catch da words an' ah'd sing it to some ol' shout song ah'd heard 'um sing from Africa, an' dey'd all take it up an' keep at it, an' keep-a addin' to it, and den it would be a spiritual.

So you see, the spirit root had taken hold," Daddy smiled, "and it was growing. Then around 1748 during a religious movement called the Great Awakening, the slave holders agreed to let missionaries and preachers from all kinds of churches come to preach to the little-tree African people and tell them of a religion called Christianity and just how they ought to take it up. The people listened to the bible stories read to them by the preachers and were amazed. It seemed as if some of the stories were about them and about how they were being mistreated in a foreign land and of how God wouldn't forget them and would help them

get away if they kept praying and believing and working for their freedom. Sometimes they were allowed to stand in the back during church services or in the balcony or just outside where they listened and memorized prayers, psalms, songs, stories and remarks the preacher read from the bible book, everything. That way they learned more new words. Later on, when they thought it was safe, they would ask a child or a traveling preacher or maybe one of their neighbors who had secretly learned to read, 'Would you please tell me, Missie (or Little Massa, or Brudder), what dis word mean?'

"For many hard and painful years they listened, watched and waited, talking with each other about the new religion. Two whispered back and forth. 'Uuum hum, they got somethin' called Baptism,' said the first one with raised eyebrows. 'Iffen you take up dey religion dat's when dey put water on you or carry you to the river water. Say after dat you belongs to dey religion.'

" 'We got somethin' like dat in our back-home religion,' answered the second one.

" 'Uuum hum,' nodded the first one. 'An' the bible book talk about a real fine place called Heaven up in the sky. Jus' the good folk go dere after dey die.'

" 'Uuumph,' the second blinked. 'Everybody talkin' heaven sure nuff ain't goin' nair, is dey? Our back-home religion got dat heaven place too. Called Orunrere.'

" 'Uuum hum,' sighed the first. 'Say dere religion got a big God go by the name Father. Say he know everythin', do anythin' and be everywhere. Say dey got saints an' angels, an' all like dat for the people to talk to. Say the big God got the power of the word.'

▼▲▼  43  ▼▲▼

" 'Hush yo' mouth,' said the second. 'Our God got dose power, an' know 'bout the word too.'

" 'Uuum hum,' agreed the first. 'Say dere big God got a little son God go by the name Jesus. Say he got a heap of praise names too, like Savior, the King of Kings, all like dat. Dey say he got the light.'

" 'Sho' nuff, weary traveler, pray,' whispered the second.

" 'Uuum hum,' rocked the first. 'Say he a friend to the downtrodden folk. The bible book say some mean folk whup him, call him out his name, shame him, put dere clothes on him, put nails in his hands an' feet, hang him up on a cross, an' make him die. An' you know what? Dey say when he die a storm come in the sky an' the thunder roll.'

" 'Oh pray,' rocked the second. 'Our God call you by the thunder. Pray.'

" 'Uuum hum, it's a sign, uuum hum,' nodded the first. 'An' couldn't no grave hold the little God's body down. Dey believe he be little an' weak but he be strong. When three days pass, he rise an' fly up in the sky to his home in heaven, Orunrere. Pray on. God is God. God never leave us. God go by many names. I do believe we ain't got long to stay here. I do believe we saved.' "

I asked Daddy, "Did they take up the new religion?"

"Little by little they did," he said. "They believed that God worked in mysterious ways and that if they took the new religion, it would be all right and they would live better. Soon they began to put some of the melodies from hymn books and names of people and places from the bible into their songs. They retold bible stories in their own way and made them work for whatever purpose they needed them for."

▼▲▼ 44 ▼▲▼

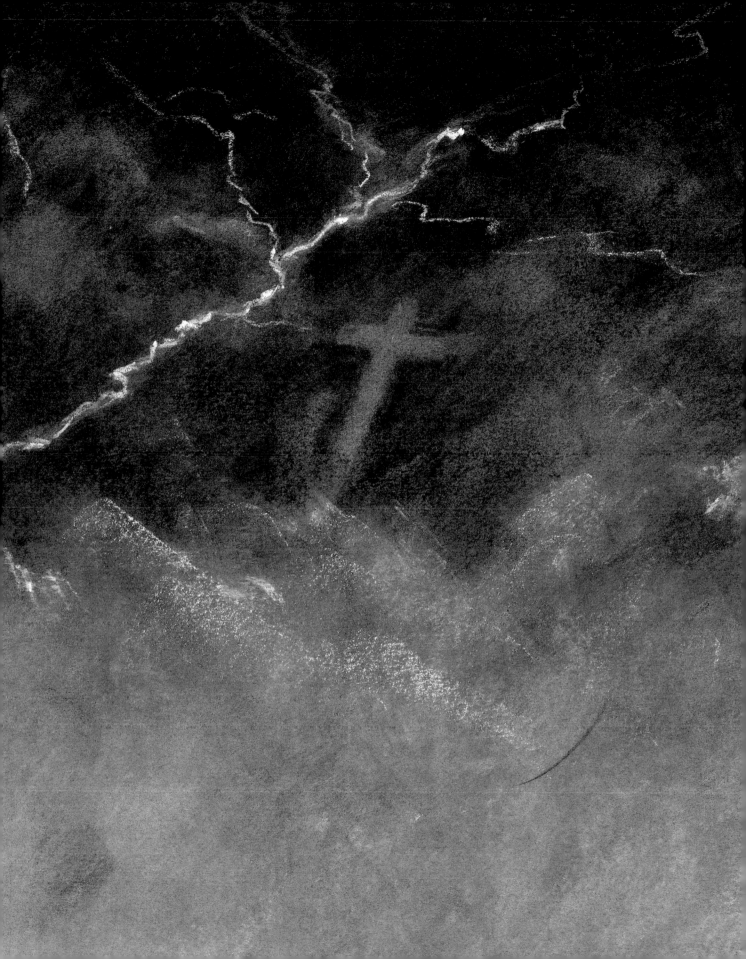

Mama leaned forward and whispered, "Sometimes to boast about
how strong they were, they would sing

> *been prayin' like Silas*
> *preachin' like Paul*
> *servin' my Lord*
> *a mighty long time*
> *an' ah ain't got weary yet.*

When they thought about their condition, sometimes they sang songs
like:

> *Sometimes ah feel like a motherless chil'*
> *a long way from home*

> or

> *Ah couldn' hear nobody pray*
> *couldn' hear nobody pray.*
> *Way down yonder by myself*
> *an' I couldn' hear nobody pray.*

To encourage one another they would sing:

> *Walk together, children. Don' you get weary.*
> *Ain't gonna let nobody turn me 'roun'.*
> *Keep-a inchin'.*
> *Keep yo' han' on the plow, hold on.*

Mr. Witherspoon put his hand up. "Yes, hold on now," he said. "I know something about that. Plenty times when the old people talked about 'home' an' 'heaven' an' 'the promised land,' they were talking about Africa or getting up north to the free states where they wouldn't be slaves nomore an' could work for pay and walk 'round much as they liked an' not have to be raggedy as jaybirds, the way they were kept in slavery. That's what my people told me down in Alabama when I was a chil'. I know plenty."

Great-Grammaw was sittin' up real tall on her folding stool. She said, "Umm hum, he do."

"And something else, children." Mr. Witherspoon leaned over to Great-Grammaw. "Those old songs were sung by that slave-stealing lady. Help me recollect her name, Sister Simpson."

"That's Harriet Tubman you're talkin' about, 'Spoon." Great-Grammaw nodded. "Umm hum."

▼▲▼  49  ▼▲▼

Mr. Witherspoon rubbed his hands together. "That's the name. You babies hear that name? Mrs. Harriet Tubman sang the spiritual songs like a sign. The first thing, she escaped from slavery herself, gone up north. The second thing, she come back down to the plantations, to the slave cabins, hiding outside in the dark night, singing the 'Steal Away' song or the 'Go Down Moses' song. When the poor African people hear that singing, they knew it meant 'Come on, I come to take you to freedom. Harriet Tubman is here.' She picks up those she could take and sets them on the Underground Railroad. That was the secret foot road leading to all the hidden places in the woods, the mountains, caves and the houses of folk who wanted freedom for the slaves, the glory road leading clear up north to sweet, sweet freedom. And Mrs. Harriet Tubman was the spiritual singing conductor on that mighty train. She took care of everything. And when the patrollers and dogs were running and chasing after Mrs. Tubman and her passengers, she would sing another spiritual song called the 'Wade in the Water' song, telling the people with her to travel in the pond or the stream or the river so's the dogs would lose track of their smell and couldn't follow up behind them nomore. She carried more than three hundred of our people out of slavery, going back year after year, from the north to the south, from the south back to the north. Praise her name. That was Mrs. Harriet Tubman."

Brother asked, "Wasn't she scared to go down to get the people?"

"Sure she was," Mr. Witherspoon told him. "But when the nose gets bopped, don't the eye cry? That means she knew she was a part of a family, and when the family was in pain she felt their pain and had to help them. And she used the spiritual songs to help her do it. Everybody knew them. By that time some of the little-tree African people were

seamstresses, carpenters, bakers, barbers, cooks, ship builders, whatever. Just like the workers in the fields, they sang spirituals too every chance they got. And it seemed like every time the slave-holding people took some of the little-tree people to their religious camp meetings back up in the woods, those little-tree African people would let loose and sing so loud the other singers had to hush up their mouths an' go to bed. Then the little-tree people would stay up all night making up and singing new spiritual songs. My dear mama told me you could hear their voices from miles away. She told me it was something. The slave-holding people started taking up their way of singing, they were so grand. Those were some days. The little tree was a-growin'."

Great-Grammaw said, "Uuum hum."

Everybody nodded, "Uuum hum."

"But they weren't finished yet." Daddy smiled. "When visitors from other countries came down to the plantations in the south, the little-tree African people would sing so beautifully for them that the visitors couldn't forget them and their songs. And when they returned to their own countries, many of the visitors talked and wrote about the spiritual songs and the people who composed and sang them. Many protested against slavery and helped the Abolitionists who were trying to stop it. And Mr. Frederick Douglass escaped from slavery, got himself together, published a newspaper, *The North Star,* and in his writing and speeches for the freedom of his people he told about how they used spirituals to ease the pain of the cruelty of slavery and as escape signals."

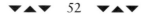

"In 1861," Mama leaned forward on her pillow and told us, "the northern states that didn't hold people in slavery went to war with the states that did. That war was called the Civil War or the War Between the States. It was happening. The little-tree African people could feel and see a change coming in their lives. They began to sing and pray more than ever. They could feel freedom in the air. Many of the men ran away and joined the Union army coming down from the north, and when they weren't fighting they were singing and composing spiritual songs. Slavery couldn't hold them anymore. Some of the women and children worked as spies for the Union army and everybody kept on singing and praying. Then on January the first in the year 1863, President Abraham Lincoln signed the Emancipation Proclamation and with that flash of the pen declared that Mr. Witherspoon's family and all the little-tree African people kept in slavery in the states still at war with the Union government were free. But the war went on for two more years. Then it came. In the year 1865 the Union soldiers won the victory and the Congress of the United States said 'yes' to the Thirteenth Amendment to the Constitution of the United States. And there it was, declared and signed to be so by law: two hundred and forty-six years after they were brought to this land, the little-tree African people were free. And oh, some hollered, some laughed, some cried, some did everything and gave thanks to God for listening to their spirit songs and prayers and for working on Mr. Lincoln and the Abolitionists. They were scared now, didn't know what was going to happen next. But they were free just like the word passed onto them from the old Africans had said they would be. No, 'the rule will not apply when the spirit won't die.' The little tree had grown in the shade."

Great-Grammaw started clappin' and we all clapped too. The people around us thought we were clappin' for the music. Then we got silly and started laughin.'

Daddy said, "That's what happened to the little-tree people when freedom came. Some of them got just plain silly. On one plantation a woman ran to the henhouse singing:

> *Rooster, don't you crow no mo',*
> *You's free, you's free.*
> *Ol' hen, don't you lay no mo' eggs,*
> *you's free, you's free.*

She ran to the pigpen:

> *Ol' pig, don't you grunt no mo',*
> *you's free, you's free.*

She ran to the cows:

> *Ol' cows, don't you give no mo' milk,*
> *you's free, you's free.*

She ran to the big house:

> *Mammy, don't you cook no mo',*
> *you's free, you's free, you's free.*

Yes, they were free, at last, and people were celebrating and planning what to do with their new freedom. On one plantation hundred-year-old Mother Carrie sat death quiet when she heard the news. For three days she went around without saying a word. On the third day, when everyone else had calmed down and was preparing to leave the plantation, old Mother Carrie recovered from her shock, let out a shout and everyone started celebrating all over again. Mother Carrie shouted:

> *"Tain't no mo' sellin' today."*
> *"No, Mother Carrie, no," the people answered.*
> *"Tain't no mo' hirin' today."*
> *"No, Mother Carrie, no."*
> *"Tain't no mo' pullin' off shirts today."*
> *"No, Mother Carrie, no."*
> *"It's stomp down freedom today."*
> *"Stomp it down."*
> *"It's stomp down freedom today."*
> *"Stomp it down."*

Brother said, "Stomp it down like a seed, Daddy?"

"Yes, son," Daddy told him. "They wanted to stomp freedom down into this land and make it live and take root and grow the way they had made themselves live and take root and grow. And they were just beginning."

That's where Daddy stopped telling the story. And he was just in time because the singer who was goin' to sing the spirituals came out on the stage. She was standin' in front of the microphone. Everybody in the audience stood up and clapped for her and the orchestra began to play. "When I was going over the old classical spiritual songs last night," she said in a soft voice, "a song came to me. I suppose you could call it a spiritual for today." Then she looked right at the people in the audience, right in our faces, and started to sing:

> *Let it be heard by all who hear*
> *we come to praise*
> *we come to praise*
> *Let it be seen by all who see*
> *we come to praise*
> *we come to praise*

> *Oh ancient seeds of royal line*
> *let us this day our souls combine*
> *and praise the love of those now gone*
> *who held our torch, who passed it on*
> *they knew our needs, they said our words*
> *they did great deeds, and would be heard*
> *we come to praise*
> *we come to praise*

Some people in the audience said "Teach" and "Praise." She sang:

> *Praise elders, worn warriors*
> *who speak the truth of history*
> *who help us stand, who help us see*
> *the greatness of our destiny*
> *we come to praise*
> *we come to praise*

"Yes, give us some praise," the elder next to us shouted.
"Praise our strong," the singer sang, "who fight with fate."
People said, "That's right."

> *to undo fear, to conquer hate*
> *They know the joy, they pray the cost*
> *when love is won, when truth is lost*
> *praise our young*

Everybody said, "Yes! Praise um! Praise us!"

> *Who lovingly keep the bond with family*
> *whose hands will hold, whose eyes will see*
> *our dreams come to reality*

Daddy and Mama and everybody stood up again clappin'. She sang:

> *Praise the love that soothes our souls,*
> *that heals our wounds, that makes us whole*
> *we come to praise*
> *we come to praise*

Everybody sang "We come to praise" with her, and after that song we sang all kinds of spirituals, fast ones, slow ones. Some of them were happy and some were sad.

Well, that's what happened at the concert. On our way home we felt good, and everybody in the street was talkin' about the singin' and the music and how it moved them. Everybody had something good to say. Everybody except Brother. He didn't say a word 'cause he was deep sleepin' on Daddy's shoulder.